The Exciting Exploits of an Effervescent Elf

by Trisha Sugarek

Baker's Plays
7611 Sunset Blvd.
Los Angeles, CA 90042
BAKERSPLAYS.COM

CHARACTERS

CHEETS – A mischievous elf. He is never still or quiet. He jumps, runs, hops, skips around the stage. He has bigger ears and feet than Donald and the other faeries. He can be played by a girl.

THOMAS – a large sea turtle. He is plodding, slow, in his movements and speech. He speaks only in nautical expressions.

STARE – The rhetorical owl.

PATSY – The spider. Plump and complacent, wants to be good but she just can't resist a free meal. Throughout the story she knits her web with gossamer yarn. The end line of the yarn is attached to the web.

EMMA – An earthling girl. She is the Queen's favorite.

DONALD – The good and kind faerie. He is in puppy love with Emma.

ROSE – Emma's mother.

MAX – The family dog, a Golden Retriever, red in color.

CLEO – Queen of the faeries, she reins over the enchanted forest and cares for the all the faeries, elves, and woodland creatures.

SCARLET, YELLOW, ORANGE, BLUE, PURPLE, GREEN – Young hand-maidens to the Queen. They are dressed in their respective colors. Long flowing gowns, reminiscent of Medieval times. Their hands, feet, hair, faces and wings are the same color as their gowns and their names.

HAZARD – King of the Underworld, he is the arch enemy of all that is good. He plans to sell the forest to developers.

HENCHMAN #1,2,3 – Soldiers of Hazard. Double cast as the land developers.

GUTTER – One of Hazard's henchman.

VARIOUS FAERIES AND SMALL CREATURES OF THE FOREST – Rabbits, skunks, squirrels, fawns, to include children of all ages in non-speaking parts.

To all the children at Dreamchasers Theatre Arts Center, Abigail, and my dear friend, Rosann

ACT I

Scene One

*(AT RISE: A lush forest. **STARE**, the owl, sits in a tree. There is a spider's web opposite. **EMMA** is trapped behind it. On a high platform sits **PATSY**, the spider, weaving and repairing the web with gossamer thread.)*

*(**CHEETS** enters, riding **THOMAS**, he urges him on as **THOMAS** slowly makes his way across the stage. **EMMA** jumps up and rushes to the side of the web so that **CHEETS** will see her.)*

CHEETS. *(agitated)* Can't this thing go any faster?? Hurry Thomas! HURRY!

THOMAS. *(plodding along)* Steady as she goes, Cheets. Don't get your rigging in a knot!

*(Hopping off **THOMAS**' back, **CHEETS** runs around.)*

CHEETS. But we must hurry! We can't find Emma anywhere and she has been missing for weeks!

STARE. Who?

CHEETS. Oh, good grief, Stare! Emma, that's 'who'!

STARE. Who?

CHEETS. EMMA!

STARE. Who?

CHEETS. Never mind! Come on, Thomas.

THOMAS. We'll find her, Matey. Stay on course and watch for a favorable wind, that's my motto.

*(**DONALD** enters. He cannot see **EMMA** in the web. **EMMA** waves at **DONALD**. **DONALD** crosses to **CHEETS** and **THOMAS**.)*

DONALD. Have you found her?

STARE. Who?

DONALD. *(unfazed by* **STARE***)* Emma.

STARE. Who?!

CHEETS. EMMA!

DONALD. STARE!

THOMAS. We've just sailed in from the windward side of the forest, Admiral. It saddens me to report, Emma was not sighted.

(While this discussion is going on, **EMMA** *is frantically waving, silently calling to them. They do not see or hear her.)*

DONALD. I was just about to scout around Emma's house once more. Thomas, could you go to the southeast corner…

*(***THOMAS*** interrupts him.)*

THOMAS. Leeward side…

DONALD. Yes, yes…go to the leeward side of the forest and ask everyone you meet if they've seen Emma.

(as **THOMAS** *turns slowly to go:)*

THOMAS. Aye, aye, Sir!

STARE. Who?

*(***THOMAS*** stops and looks up at **STARE**.)*

THOMAS. And, you there! Keep a sharp eye out from the poop deck.

CHEETS. Hurry, Thomas!

THOMAS. Huh?

(at his turtle's pace)

Oh, yes. Steady on course.

(As **THOMAS** *exits, he mumbles.)*

A clean bottom adds hull speed. Over the side you scurvy nere'do wells. You, there, in the crow's nest, has land been sighted? …Unfurl the foresail…more speed.

*(***CHEETS*** and **DONALD** *watch as* **THOMAS** *exits.)*

DONALD. Now, to business. Are you certain, Cheets, that you have talked to everyone?

CHEETS. Of course! Cheets is the smartest elf in the forest. Do you know how you can tell?

DONALD. Yes, *(sighs)* I've heard it all before…bigger ears…

(**CHEETS** *interrupts.*)

CHEETS. …better to hear with,

(wiggling his generous ears)

Bigger feet…

(**CHEETS** *lifts a good sized foot to demonstrate.*)

…better to run with…bigger brains…

DONALD. …yes, I know! Better to think with… So get those brains working and find Emma! I'm off now, we'll meet back here tomorrow.

(**DONALD** *exits walking by* **EMMA.** **EMMA** *reacts.* **CHEETS** *starts to follow him and stops in shock. There is* **EMMA** *right before his eyes.* **CHEETS** *does a backward summersault, rubs his eyes, and looks at* **EMMA** *again.*)

CHEETS. Emma?

STARE. Who??

CHEETS. *(delighted)* EMMA!!

STARE. WHO!!

(**CHEETS** *rushes over to* **EMMA.**)

CHEETS. Emma, what happened? What are you doing in there? Emma! Can you hear me?

(**EMMA** *is talking but* **CHEETS** *cannot hear her.* **PATSY,** *the spider, giggles mischievously. To* **PATSY.**)

Who are you?

STARE. Who??

CHEETS. Stare! Be quiet! *(to* **PATSY***)* Who *are* you?

PATSY. I'm Patsy, the Banana Spider.

(**PATSY** *sits, complacent, knitting new strands for her web. She munches bugs from a basket by her side.*)

STARE. Who?

PATSY. I'm Patsy…

CHEETS. Don't! If you keep answering Stare, we'll be here all day! Where did you come from? I've never seen you in our forest before.

PATSY. Duh! I came in on a load of bananas, silly! Liked what I saw so decided to stay. Your bugs are particularly tasty here in this forest. I wonder why that is… *(Beat. Munches more bugs.)* Could it be the sun at this latitude? Perhaps the water…

*(Frustrated, **CHEETS** jumps around.)*

CHEETS. I DON'T CARE WHY THE BUGS ARE BETTER TASTING HERE!! I must ask that you release my friend immediately!

STARE. Who?

*(Forgets himself and answers **STARE**.)*

CHEETS. EMMA!!

PATSY. *(unfazed)* I'm afraid I can't do that.

CHEETS. At once!

PATSY. Nope.

CHEETS. Why not? What's Emma ever done to you?

PATSY. Nothing. She's seems very nice.

STARE. Who?

PATSY. Emma.

CHEETS. Stare!!

Then you must let her go. I insist!

*(**EMMA** is waving and silently gesturing to **CHEETS** to get his attention. **CHEETS** crosses to **EMMA**.)*

Don't worry, Emma. I'll have you out of there in no time or my name isn't Cheets!

*(**EMMA** starts gesturing again.)*

CHEETS *(cont.)* What?

STARE. Who?

CHEETS. Stare, for the last time, shush! Be quiet, desist, silence! Emma, I can't hear you!

(EMMA *gestures and points to* PATSY *as if to say, 'Ask her.'*)

What?…Oh! Ask the spider?

(EMMA *vigorously nods her head.*)

Okay! Bananas, what's Emma doing?…

STARE. Who?

PATSY. My name is Patsy! Banana spider is what I *am*. Really!!

CHEETS. Okay, *Patsy*! What's going on? Release my friend right now!

PATSY. Sorry, no can do.

CHEETS. Why not?

PATSY. Got a deal.

CHEETS. With who?

STARE. *(trying to join in)* Who?

PATSY. With Hazard. Ever heard of him?

STARE. Who?

(*in fear*)

CHEETS. Hazard??

STARE. Whoooooo?

PATSY. Yep. All the flies, moths, lady bugs, cock roaches that I want. And my personal favorite, lightnin' bugs… umm…They fizzle as they go down! Yummy!!…

CHEETS. Enough with the bugs!!

PATSY. Excuse me!…As I was saying, all I want, fresh daily, if I sit here and keep my web in good repair and make certain your friend does not escape.

(PATSY *knits furiously.*)

CHEETS. But, why? Why does Hazard want Emma kept captive?

PATSY. Don't know, don't care.

CHEETS. Well, shame on you Patsy!

PATSY. I know…*(sighs)* …it's very bad of me. I don't have anything against your friend…whats'er name…

CHEETS. Emma.

STARE. Who?

PATSY. *(cont.)* Yes, Emma. But, all those lovely bugs, delivered every day? Yum, it was impossible to say no.

CHEETS. Well, that's very greedy of you! And greed makes you ugly.

(**PATSY** *continues knitting.* **EMMA** *waves her arms and silently calls to* **CHEETS.** *He crosses to her.* **CHEETS** *attempts to break the web with his hands.)*

Cheets is trying, Emma. This greedy spider won't release you and I can't *(groans)* break the web. Oh, Emma, I don't know what we're going to do. I can't get you free. Nothing is working.

(**EMMA** *gestures.* **CHEETS** *places his hands around his ears to show that he can't hear her. In a loud voice.)*

I. CAN'T. HEAR. YOU.

(**EMMA** *begins to pantomime. As* **EMMA** *gestures,* **CHEETS** *guesses at what she is saying.* **EMMA** *gestures: first word, two syllables, etc.)*

Okay. First word, two syllables.

(**EMMA** *begins to pantomime a big scary monster.)*

Scary. Big. A bear…an elephant?…No. Too many syllables. A TROLL?…Don't tell me the Troll is back. The Queen will be very displeased.

(**EMMA** *vigorously shakes her head.)*

STARE. Who?

(**EMMA** *demonstrates someone who is very arrogant; hands on hips she struts around.)*

CHEETS. Proud. Big shot! Donald?

(**EMMA** *glares at* **CHEETS.** *)*

Oh! Hazard? Patsy said Hazard captured you but you can't believe such a greedy spider now can you? The minute she said it was Hazard Cheets scoffed at her, Emma, I really did…Cheets is very brave…

(**EMMA** *stamps her foot and silently motions* **CHEETS** *to be quiet.*)

CHEETS. *(cont.)* But why, Emma? What does Hazard want?

STARE. Who?

(**EMMA** *nods several times, places her finger on her own nose to indicate 'on the nose.' She gestures: two words.*)

CHEETS. Two words.

(**EMMA** *points to her wrist for a watch and the time.*)

Watch? Minute? No? Hour? Okay, hour.

(**EMMA** *gestures all around pointing to the forest.*)

Green? Tree, sky, bush? all together, oh! Forest. Hour Forest? Hour forest? OH! *OUR* FOREST.

(**EMMA** *touches her nose; very excited.*)

What about it?

(**EMMA** *begins stomping, slashing, waving her arms about, making chopping motions. Misunderstanding,* **CHEETS** *grabs hold of the web and shakes it.*)

I can't break it free, Emma. It's too strong.

(**EMMA** *shakes her head. She whirls around trying to tell* **CHEETS** *it's bigger than getting her free. It's about the forest.*)

It's not about breaking the web?

PATSY. As if you could!

CHEETS. Okay, it's about our forest.

(**CHEETS** *paces around in circles, glancing at* **EMMA** *every so often.*)

Emma is stomping in our forest, slashing with a sword?

(**EMMA** *now swaggers around to represent* **HAZARD.***)

Hazard is slashing with a sword?

(**EMMA** *indicates yes and again indicates the entire forest.*)

Hazard…

STARE. Who?

CHEETS. *(to* **STARE***) Quiet!...... (to* **EMMA***)* Hazard is going to cut our trees?!

(**EMMA** *indicates "on the nose." She measures a imaginary board, marks it, cuts it, hammers a nail into it. Repeats it again while* **CHEETS** *watches.)*

Cutting? Hammer, nails? Then another one? Hazard is going to build something here...

(**EMMA** *gestures"on the nose." She pantomimes a house and opening and walking into the house. She pantomimes many houses.)*

A house. Hazard is building his castle here?

(**EMMA** *shakes her head "no." She gestures four syllables.)*

Four syllables? Okay.

(**EMMA** *gestures a submarine submerging into the sea.)*

A boat. A sinking boat? No?

(She gestures a sailor at a periscope in a submarine.)

A boat under the water...a periscope? A submarine? Yes! A submarine!

(**EMMA** *nods and gestures to shorten the word.)*

Short word for submarine. Sub!

(**EMMA** *gestures second word.)*

Second word.

(**EMMA** *starts to work a division math problem.)*

Adding? Substraction! No. *Division!*

(**EMMA** *vigorously nods and silently claps her hands. She gestures to put the two words together. She pantomimes a house again and then flashes ten fingers over and over to indicate dozens, hundreds of houses.)*

Sub-division. What's a sub-division?

(As quickly as **EMMA** *gestures,* **CHEETS** *yells out words.)*

A house. A big house. One house? Two, three, ten? Forty?

(**EMMA** *gestures wildly that it is more.*)

More than forty? One hundred? More? Oh, Emma that can't be right! That would mean our beautiful, magical forest would disappear! Are you certain?

(**EMMA** *nods. She points at* **CHEETS** *to imply that he must do something about it. She gestures to get everyone; Donald and the Queen by describing them in pantomime.*)

(**CHEETS** *puffs out his chest and struts around.*)

Cheets must DO something!

STARE. Who?

PATSY. HA!

CHEETS. Donald? Yes, yes. And….

(**EMMA** *continues to gesture.*)

The Queen. Yes! Yes! Tell Donald and the Queen! They will know what to do. Cheets will help….

(**DONALD** *enters with* **CLEO**, *Queen of the Faeries, and her* **HANDMAIDENS**. *All the woodland creatures are peeking out from behind trees and bushes.*)

CHEETS. *(cont.)* Donald! I found Emma!

(*Belatedly,* **CHEETS** *makes a courtly bow to the* **QUEEN**.)

Queen Cleo! Your servant!

DONALD. You found her? Where? Where is she??

STARE. Who? Who?

(**CHEETS** *stalks over to* **STARE**'s *tree in a menacing manner.* **DONALD** *snags* **CHEETS** *by the arm.*)

DONALD. No time for that, Cheets. Where is Emma?

(**CHEETS** *skips and runs over to the spider web.*)

CHEETS. Why…right here. She can hear us…But you can't hear her. *(boasting)* Cheets is the only one who can talk to her…Cheets is very…

(**DONALD** *interrupts.*)

DONALD. Where?

CHEETS. Where what?

STARE. Who?

DONALD. Where is Emma?

>   (*Jumping up and down in front of the web and pointing at* **EMMA**)

CHEETS. Right here!!

QUEEN CLEO. Cheets, this is no time for one of your pranks! Where is Emma?

STARE. Who??

CHEETS. She's right there.

DONALD. Where?

STARE. Who?

QUEEN CLEO. Where?

CHEETS. THERE!!

>   (*All stand staring at each other for a beat. Silence.*)

PATSY. Oh…this is such fun!

>   (**PATSY** *pops a handful of bugs into her mouth and continues to knit.*)

CHEETS. You. Can't. See. Her?

>   (**THOMAS** *enters stage right.*)

THOMAS. Thar' she blows!!

CHEETS. Thomas, thank goodness! You see her?!

THOMAS. Who?

STARE. Who?

CHEETS. Emma! You see her, right?

THOMAS. Who, Emma?

CHEETS. Emma, Thomas. You said, 'thar she blows'…

THOMAS. My dear boy! That's an expression used at sea when you see whales…Since everyone is gathered here, I thought it appropriate.

CHEETS. (*looking at everyone*) None of you can see her? She's right there.

>   (**CHEETS** *runs up to the web.* **EMMA** *waves at everyone.*)

DONALD. This joke is in poor taste, Cheets. We're all very worried about Emma.

CHEETS. But…*(running around the stage, stopping at several woodland creatures)* You must see her…she's right there!

QUEEN CLEO. Cheets, do you need a time out?

*(**CHEETS** stops in front of the **QUEEN**.)*

CHEETS. Your Majesty, ask the spider. Ask Patsy!

STARE. Who?

THOMAS. Yes! Put Patsy on the stand. We can hold a marine court-martial right here. I will be the judge!

*(**QUEEN CLEO** and her **HANDMAIDENS** cross to where **PATSY** is knitting away. As **CLEO** passes, **EMMA** curtsies.)*

QUEEN CLEO. Miss Patsy, we understand that you might be able to shed some light on Emma's disappearance?

PATSY. *(shrugs)* I could.

(beat)

QUEEN CLEO. Well?

PATSY. If I wanted to. But, alas, I don't…want to.

QUEEN CLEO. Do you know who we are?

STARE. Who?

DONALD. Quiet.

CHEETS. Stare!

QUEEN CLEO. We are the royal court of this forest and rule all who live here. I am Queen Cleo, Queen of the Faeries.

*(**PATSY** knits and munches, unfazed by **QUEEN CLEO**'s importance.)*

Do you know what that means?

PATSY. Let's see…do I care? Nooo!

*(All gasp at **PATSY**'s rudeness.)*

QUEEN CLEO. We can banish you!

PATSY. If you banish me, how will you get Emma back?

*(**CHEETS** runs toward **PATSY** as if to attack her. **DONALD** grabs him.)*

CHEETS. Lemme' at her. I'll make her talk. *She* can see Emma. She's right there, trapped in Patsy's web.

(*holding* **CHEETS** *back*)

DONALD. Cheets, stop! Calm yourself!

QUEEN CLEO. Cheets. There's no one there. It's just an old, ordinary spider web...

(*insulted*)

PATSY. Hey!!

(**CHEETS** *breaks away from* **DONALD** *and runs up to* **EMMA** *behind the web.*)

CHEETS. Emma! Wave your arms, jump around, show them all where you are!!

(**EMMA** *complies.*)

DONALD. (*sadly*) Cheets, there's no one there.

THOMAS. Steady as she blows!

STARE. Who?

(*to her* **HANDMAIDENS**)

QUEEN CLEO. Scarlet! Marine! Ochre! Forest! Can you see anyone in the web?

(*The* **HANDMAIDENS** *shake their heads.* **CHEETS** *sits on the toad stool and puts his head in his bands.*)

CHEETS. Oh, Emma, what are we going to do?

THOMAS. Every day you landlubbers believe in things you can't see. For example, all seafaring creatures, such as myself, live in a glorious blue ocean. You have not 'seen' it but you believe we live there. If Cheets says Emma is here, well then, by great jumping dolphins, she's here. I believe Cheets! Emma is here.

(**THOMAS** *plods over to the web and while he cannot see* **EMMA,** *he speaks to her.*)

Hello, Emma. We'll get you off those slippery decks in no time. Just keep your back to the wind until we sight land.

Scene Two

*(AT RISE: **PATSY** sits knitting her web; **EMMA** sits on a toad stool resting her chin on her hand. **CHEETS, DONALD, STARE,** and other woodland creatures and faeries flutter about. As someone approaches, they fade into the forest and watch. **CHEETS** is wearing an elaborate knitted cap covered in twigs and leaves.)*

*(**ROSE, EMMA**'s mother, enters. She is accompanied by **MAX,** the family Golden Retriever dog. **MAX** rushes ahead of **ROSE** and crosses to **PATSY**'s web. He can see **EMMA.** His tail is wagging furiously and he barks a welcome.)*

ROSE. Max! Come here! Don't go too far.

*(**MAX** ignores her, intent on **EMMA.**)*

Max! Get away from that! Come here, boy!

*(**ROSE** sits on a log. **MAX** crosses back to **ROSE** and sits at her knee.)*

Good boy!

*(**ROSE** is sad and worried. She begins to weep quietly. **EMMA** rises and goes to the web where she can see her mother. **EMMA** gestures but cannot be heard. **MAX** whines a greeting.)*

What is it, Max?

STARE. Who?

ROSE. It's just an old nasty spider web, Max. Stay here.

*(**MAX** whines.)*

PATSY. Well! I never!

CHEETS. *(to **DONALD**)* Who is that?

STARE. Who?

DONALD. I believe it's Emma's mother. I saw her once from the edge of the forest, hanging out the laundry.

CHEETS. You went to Emma's house?

DONALD. I was waiting for Emma to come out.

CHEETS. Why is she here? This is not good. Look! She's crying. Oh, dear, oh dear!

DONALD. I'll go and speak with her.

CHEETS. Wait! You might frighten her. She'll never understand your ears.

DONALD. I don't care. She must be very worried about Emma. Why else would she be here?

STARE. Who?

(CHEETS *and* DONALD *both "shush"* STARE.)

CHEETS. Well, you can't go out there like that…*(thinks a minute)* I know!

(CHEETS *takes his cap off and pulls it over* DONALD*'s head down enough to cover the tops of his pointed ears.*)

There! That'll do the job!

(DONALD *starts to cross.*)

Wait! Take off your shoes!

DONALD. Why?

CHEETS. Because they are a dead-give-away that you're a faerie.

DONALD. I resent that! Just because you think elves are better than faeries, we have you beat in shoe fashion.

CHEETS. That's a matter of opinion!

(*They begin a nonsense argument about shoes and style.* ROSE, EMMA*'s mother rises as if to leave.*)

DONALD. Oh yeah? More than one person thinks your shoes are ridiculous!

CHEETS. What? My shoes are stupendous…..

(*Suddenly they notice* ROSE *begin to leave.*)

Oh! Oh! she's leaving!!

STARE. Who?

CHEETS. Get out there!

(CHEETS *pushes* DONALD *out into the clearing where* ROSE *can see him.* DONALD *bows to* ROSE.*)

DONALD. Please have no fear Lady. I am Donald, Emma's friend.

ROSE. Donald? But…but…you're not real! You're Emma's imaginary playmate…aren't you?

DONALD. Ah! Then Emma has told you of me?

ROSE. Yes, when she goes to play in the forest, she says that she is going to meet 'Donald.' I just assumed that you were imaginary because none of the families we know around here have a son named Donald.

DONALD. I assure you, Lady, I am very real.

ROSE. Where do you live?

DONALD. On the very far side of this forest…a great distance from your farm.

ROSE. Oh, Donald! Emma is missing. Do you know where she is? I am so frightened that she has been hurt.

DONALD. I am sorry to say that we…*(coughs)* …that is…*I* do not know. We've…I mean, *I* have been looking for her these many weeks.

ROSE. The police and the FBI haven't found out anything. It's like Emma has disappeared into thin air. I'm so frightened!

(**CHEETS** *runs out of the trees, unable to tolerate* **ROSE***'s pain.*)

CHEETS. Lady! Lady!

DONALD. Cheets, NO !!

STARE. Who?

ROSE. Who?

(**CHEETS** *skids to a stop in front of* **ROSE,** *almost running into her.*)

CHEETS. I KNOW! CHEETS KNOWS! CHEETS KNOWS WHERE EMMA IS!!

DONALD. Cheets, You're going to scare Emma's mother away. You don't know any such thing!

(**ROSE** *takes* **CHEETS** *by the hand and crosses to the stool and sits.*)

ROSE. Hello, Cheets. Emma has spoken of you often…But, like Donald, I thought you were imaginary…

CHEETS. Cheets *is not* imaginary! Cheets is very real. Cheets is an elf with the most handsome shoes. Cheets is much smarter and faster than any ol' faerie!

ROSE. I am sure that is very true, Cheets. But, you must admit, Donald is very nice too. Don't you think?

CHEETS. Well…

DONALD. I am sorry, Lady, Cheets gets carried away.

CHEETS. I do not! Cheets is smart, fast…

STARE. Who?

ROSE. Now, Cheets, what's this about Emma? Do you really know where she is?

CHEETS. Yes, Lady, I do.

(He jumps up and crosses to PATSY*'s web. Indicates* EMMA.*)*

See? Emma's right here! You just can't see or hear her. Only I, Cheets the elf, can see her.

*(*MAX *rises, tail wagging, and barks at* EMMA.*)*

ROSE. Where, Cheets? I don't see anything except a spider web…*(She shudders.)*…a very large spider web.

PATSY. Thank you.

CHEETS. She's right there!!

*(*EMMA *is jumping up and down on the other side of the web and* CHEETS *mimics her actions on his side of the web.)*

ROSE. Where? Oh, Cheets! Is this some kind of cruel joke?

DONALD. No, Lady. Cheets has been telling us for a week now that Emma is trapped behind the spider's web. He even talks to her. But, like you, we can't see her. We all think it is one of Cheets' tall tales.

CHEETS. Is not! IS NOT! Cheets doesn't have any tall tales. Emma is right there.

*(*MAX *crosses to the web, looks at* EMMA *and barks.)*

ROSE. No, no! Of course you don't lie. You wouldn't lie to me, Emma's mother, would you, Cheets?

CHEETS. Cheets doesn't lie! I will prove it! Ask me a question for Emma; something that only you and Emma know the answer to.

DONALD. Cheets, that's enough…this is ridiculous. Only *you* can see Emma? I am, after all, her best friend. Why can't I see her?

CHEETS. I don't know. *(beat)* Go ahead, Lady, ask me a question.

(All the faeries and woodland creatures start to come out and sit quietly, observing the scene.)

ROSE. All right. Ask Emma…*(beat)* What did I sing to her when she was a baby and she couldn't go to sleep.

*(Even though **CHEETS** has turned to **EMMA** as if to repeat the question, **EMMA** can hear. **EMMA** immediately starts pantomiming her answer. **EMMA** indicates first word, then places her finger to her lips to indicate 'hush'.)*

CHEETS. Okay, Emma. First word.

ROSE. What are you doing?

CHEETS. I can't hear Emma so she pantomimes what she wants me to know…*(**CHEET**'s attention returns to **EMMA**.)*

ROSE. Like Charades?

STARE. Who?

ROSE. *(to **STARE**)* Charades. It's a 'what' not a 'who.'

CHEETS. Exactly!

"Sh…sh…"

*(**EMMA** shakes her head no.)*

"Be quiet"?

*(Again, **EMMA** gestures no.)*

DONALD. *(to **CHEETS**)* Try 'Hush'.

CHEETS. *(indignant)* I was just going to say that. 'Hush"?

*(**EMMA** nods her head. And indicates second word two syllables and then, with her fingers close together, for 'little'.)*

CHEETS. *(cont.)* Small? Tiny?

> (**EMMA** *shakes her head and with her fingers emphasizing 'little'.*)

Little!

> (**EMMA** *nods and gestures for the third word, cradling a baby in her arms.*)

Baby? 'Hush little baby'?

> (**EMMA** *places her index finger on the tip of her nose. Then indicates fourth word 'don't' and points at* **CHEETS** *for 'you' and mimes someone crying.*)

NO? Don't? Doesn't? Okay, fourth word is 'don't? Next word is me. NO? Oh, YOU! Next word is crying?

> (**ROSE** *begins to sing the Mockingbird nursery rhyme.*)

ROSE. 'Hush little baby don't you cry, Mama's goin' buy you a mockin' bird and if that mockin' bird don't sing, Mama's goin' buy you a diamond ring....

> (**ROSE** *rushes over to the web. Clings to it. Even though she cannot see* **EMMA**, **ROSE** *talks to her.*)

Oh! Emma, my darling girl. It's Mama! Can she hear me Cheets?

CHEETS. Yes, Lady, she can.

ROSE. How do we get her out?

DONALD. Can you see her, Lady?

ROSE. No, I can't, Donald. But I believe Cheets. No one knows what I sang to Emma except Emma and I. It was long ago.

DONALD. But none of us can see her, Lady.

> (**DONALD** *indicates all the faeries and creatures from the forest gathered around.* **ROSE** *looks around her in amazement.*)

ROSE. I don't need to *see* Emma to believe she's there. We can't see the wind, but we feel it and believe. You can't see the air but you breath it...you can't *see* love but you believe in it and want to be loved..

(All twitter in agreement with each other.)

ROSE. *(cont.)* Donald, Cheets, how do we get her free?

DONALD. Patsy won't tell us.

ROSE. Who?

STARE. Who?

CHEETS. Patsy, that very greedy spider up there.

> *(***ROSE*** *looks up and sees* **PATSY**. *She crosses over to stand under her.)*

ROSE. Hello, Patsy. How do you do? I'm Emma's mother, Rose.

> *(***MAX*** *has walked beside* **ROSE** *and growls up at* **PATSY**. **PATSY** *pops another bug into her mouth and grins down at* **ROSE**.*)*

PATSY. Humph! So what?

ROSE. There's no need to be rude. Didn't your mother teach you any manners?

PATSY. My mother had one hundred and thirteen of us kids. She really didn't have time for teaching good 'manners'!

ROSE. Won't you please set Emma free?

PATSY. Why should I? You called my web ugly and nasty… not very good manners if you ask me.

ROSE. I am so sorry, Patsy. When I look closer it is actually very lovely.

PATSY. Do you have any idea how brilliant my design is? How beautifully executed? How long it takes? How unique each and every web is…have you never seen how it sparkles when the rain drops are caught in it?

> *(***DONALD*** *crosses to* **PATSY**.*)*

DONALD. Yes, yes, Patsy, you have been telling us almost nonstop. We think it is wonderful but please! Emma doesn't belong in your web.

ROSE. Yes, please release her.

PATSY. Sorry. Can't do it. Got a deal.

ROSE. A deal? With who?

STARE. Whom?

PATSY. Him!

ROSE. Who?

STARE. Who?

DONALD. Hazard, my Lady. King of the Underworld.

ROSE. But why?

CHEETS. My Lady, Emma has told me, Cheets the elf, what Hazard plans. I think he has taken Emma captive so she can't interfere with those plans.

DONALD. Yes, Cheets says that Emma told him that Hazard is selling the forest to builders…

ROSE. But…

CHEETS. Donald! It's my story to tell the Lady.

DONALD. Okay, then get on with it.

CHEETS. Emma says that Hazard is going to sell the forest to builders who are going to build dozens, no, *hundreds* of houses.

(*All the faeries and woodland creatures show their concern.* **STARE** *flaps his wings.*)

ROSE. But the forest is on my land. It's part of my farm and has been in my family for hundreds of years.

DONALD. Yes, we know, Lady. But before earthlings came to our forest, we had been here for *centuries*. We are reigned over by Cleo, Queen of the faeries.

ROSE. Oh, my goodness, all of the stories that Emma has told me are not made up? I thought she just had a very creative imagination. But you say it's all true?

DONALD. Yes, my Lady.

ROSE. Oh my.

ALL. Oh my.

Scene Three

*(AT RISE: The forest. **PATSY**, the spider munches and knits, the faeries romp and play, the woodland creatures hide and seek, **STARE** watches from his perch. **EMMA** sits inside the web, chin resting on her hand. **DONALD** and **CHEETS** sit quietly talking just outside the web, near **EMMA**.)*

*(**THOMAS** enters far upstage. Plodding down stage, he continues and on his line about changing course he crosses, left to **DONALD** and **CHEETS**.)*

THOMAS. Lower the main to half! Furl the foresail! Helmsman, change course three points starboard. *(He changes course himself.)* You there, in the crow's nest, any enemy ships on the horizon?

*(**THOMAS** arrives near **CHEETS** and **DONALD**.)*

Ahoy, mates! Have we landed? Is Emma free?

DONALD. No, Thomas, sadly Emma is still captive.

STARE. Who?

CHEETS. Patsy is the most stubborn spider I have ever met. She will not budge!

PATSY. Humpf!

STARE. Who?

DONALD. Stare, please!

THOMAS. Man the cannon! Load and fire at will!

PATSY. Eek! He's got guns?

DONALD. No, Patsy, it's just the way he talks. There are no guns in our forest.

PATSY. I should hope NOT!

(off)

CHORUS. Behold! His Royal Majesty, King Hazard comes. Make Way!

STARE. Who?

*(All the faeries and woodland creatures scatter. **DONALD** and **CHEETS** rise. **THOMAS** slowly turns in the direction of **HAZARD**'s entrance. **EMMA** rises. **PATSY** munches and knits.)*

THOMAS. It's an ill wind blowin'. Freebooters approaching on the port side. All hands on deck!

CHEETS. He's coming! Hazard arrives. Lemme' at 'em. He'll be sorry he took our Emma when Cheets gets through with him! The villain! On guard!

DONALD. Cheets, quiet. Let's see if we can talk to Hazard. That's always the best way.

THOMAS. Time's past for talking, dance the hempen jig…

(Thunder claps, lightning flashes as **HAZARD** *and his* **ENTOURAGE** *enter.* **HENCHMEN** *cross behind* **HAZARD**. *He is dressed in a handsome suit and tie with a modest 'business' style crown on his head. He carries a briefcase.)*

HENCHMEN. Clear the way. King Hazard approaches!

*(**HAZARD** looks at **EMMA**.)*

HAZARD. Well, well, well, our little troublemaker is very quiet this morning. *(to **PATSY**)* Good work, Patsy.

PATSY. Thank you, your Majesty.

*(**HAZARD** turns away.)*

Ahem, if it pleases your Majesty, I am running low on lightning bugs. And I need five more skeins of gossamer.

HAZARD. *(**HAZARD** indicates to one of his henchmen.)* Make a note, Gutter.

*(The **HENCHMAN** gets out a note pad and pen.)*

GUTTER. Yes, Sire.

PATSY. Oh! And some lady bugs, the red kind. They are much spicier here in your forest…much better than at home…

HAZARD. *(losing patience)* Yes, yes. More lady bugs for Patsy, Gutter.

GUTTER. Yes, Sire, right away, Sire.

*(The **HENCHMEN** exit.)*

HAZARD. Now to business. *(beat)* Greetings, underlings and creatures. I have a very important appointment this morning and you must all vacate my forest.

CHEETS. VACATE!? VACATE! Oh my, what does it mean?

DONALD. It means we have to leave, Cheets.

> (**CHEETS** *runs around.*)

CHEETS. But where will we all go? What about my carrots? And what does he mean, 'my forest'. It's our forest and of course Queen Cleo and oh, *(glances at* **EMMA***)* Emma's forest if we want to get technical…

THOMAS. Prepare to be boarded…

HAZARD. Silence!!

STARE. Whom?

HAZARD. Him!

CHEETS. Me!

DONALD. (**DONALD** *is not afraid.*) You can't order us to leave, Hazard. The forest belongs to Emma and her mother. The Queen ordered it so.

HAZARD. Bah! Cleo can't give my forest to any mere earthlings! Whoever heard of such a thing.

STARE. Whom.

CHEETS. *(crosses to* **STARE***)* No, Stare, I'm pretty sure it's 'whoever' not 'whomever'.

THOMAS. I believe it's whomever. It has to do with pronouns and the like. Very choppy waters, if you ask me.

CHEETS. No, Cheets knows! It's 'whoever'.

DONALD. Is it 'whomever'? Stare is, after all, our expert on the word.

STARE. Who?

CHEETS. You!

DONALD. You!

THOMAS. Stare.

HAZARD. *QUIET! (He bellows.)* I can't think!

> (**ROSE** *enters with* **MAX** *at her side. As she passes the web she throws a kiss to* **EMMA**. **ROSE** *does not notice* **HAZARD** *and his immediate and shocked reaction to her.* **ROSE** *crosses to stand with* **DONALD**.*)

ROSE. Oh, Donald, I am so pleased to have found you this morning. Good morning, Cheets.

(**DONALD** *bows deeply.*)

DONALD. Lady Rose, Good morn to you.

(*Delighted,* **CHEETS** *runs in circles around* **ROSE**.)

CHEETS. Good morning, Lady! Cheets is here, Cheets is your servant, your knight in shining armor! Just tell me what I may do to be of service to you!

ROSE. *(fondly)* Thank you, Cheets. Do you have any messages for me?

CHEETS. Yes, Lady. Emma says to tell you she misses you very much.

(**ROSE** *crosses to the web. She speaks to* **EMMA** *even though she cannot see her.*)

ROSE. I miss you too, Emma dear.

(**ROSE** *turns again to* **DONALD**.)

Donald, have you found a way to free her?

DONALD. No, my Lady, not as yet…

(**HAZARD** *crosses to* **ROSE**. **MAX** *growls at him.*)

HAZARD. My Lady, may I present myself?

(**ROSE** *turns to him and is very still.*)

I am King Hazard. And you are my own, Lady Roselyn. *(beat)* It's been a very long time.

ROSE. *(puzzled)* I am afraid you are mistaken, Your Majesty, we have never met. I would remember. My name is Rose and my daughter, Emma, is missing.

HAZARD. *(stumbles)* Your daughter? Missing? I…I had no idea.

ROSE. Yes. Do you know her, sir?

PATSY. HA!

STARE. Who?

HAZARD. No, dear Lady, I don't.

DONALD. Hazard, you…

(**CHEETS** *runs around the stage, shouting.*)

CHEETS. Fibber! He's a fibber! Lord Hazard is telling fibs…

HAZARD. SILENCE!

(**HAZARD** *starts after* **CHEETS**. **CHEETS** *runs off.* **HAZARD** *turns back to* **ROSE**.)

Queen of my heart, my love. We have met many times. I have loved you for over four centuries and now, here in this forest,

(**HAZARD** *kneels on one knee like a gallant of olden days.*)

I have found you again. I thought…I thought you were lost to me forever.

(**ROSE** *changes. She becomes very still. All sweetness and gentleness is gone. She speaks in a regal voice.*)

ROSE. RISE AND BE GONE! AWAY WITH YOU, HAZARD! Take your jewels, your land, castles, horses and gowns with you!

HAZARD. Please, Roselyn, listen to me. I did not kill your husband king.

ROSE. You dare? *(beat)* You *DARE* to stand there and deny your evil actions that caused the death of my beloved?

HAZARD. I swear upon my love for you. I. HAD. NOTH-ING. TO. DO. WITH. YOUR. KING'S. DEATH.

(**HAZARD** *rises. Humble.*)

Do not send me away…again.

ROSE. I want NOTHING to do with you! Not then, not now, not EVER!

Intermission

ACT II

Scene One

(AT RISE: Seconds later.)

*(**DONALD** crosses to **ROSE**'s side. **MAX** whines and growls. **ROSE** comes back to herself. Everyone is shocked by her response.)*

DONALD. Lady Rose, are you well?

ROSE. Yes, darling Donald. I am quite well. I don't know what came over me just now. The words seem to spill out of my mouth. It was the most extraordinary feeling.

HAZARD. Doesn't that prove to you that we have known each other? That I have loved only you for centuries?

ROSE. It proves nothing, Your Majesty. I am sorry but I do not know you. I suspect that I am upset about my daughter being caught in that web. Please do not speak to me in that manner again.

HAZARD. Oh yes, the girl. She is your daughter, Roselyn, truly?

ROSE. She is. *(beat)* Do you know something you are not telling me, Lord Hazard?

HAZARD. Perhaps after my '*business meeting*' I too can help you.

DONALD. Don't listen to him, Lady…he is not to be trusted.

THOMAS. Throw 'em in the brig.

*(**CHEETS** enters at a run, rushing around but avoiding getting close to **HAZARD**.)*

CHEETS. Hazard is a fibber. Beware! Fibber! Fibber! Pants on fire!

*(**HAZARD** starts after **CHEETS** then remembers **ROSE** and stops. He returns to **ROSE**'s side.)*

HAZARD. Please forgive me, Roselyn, but that little green… *thing*…can be very annoying.

ROSE. I find him adorable.

HAZARD. Yes, yes of course. Adorable. But, I must excuse myself from your presence. I have pressing business. Farewell…for now.

(**HAZARD** *takes* **ROSE**'s *hand and kisses it.* **ROSE** *pulls away.* **HAZARD** *exits.*)

ROSE. What a strange man. *(beat)* Donald, what do you know of him?

STARE. Who?

ROSE. *(to* **STARE***)* His Majesty, Lord Hazard.

THOMAS. Don't be hornswoggled by the likes of 'em, my Lady.

DONALD. He is a bad man, Lady. He has lived for centuries and rules the dark side of the forest. Queen Cleo banished him from this forest because he put a curse on Prince Rainier, turning him into a bewitched unicorn…

(There is the sound of music, horns and bells and great fanfare.)

Oh! The Queen cometh, Lady.

THOMAS. Thar' she blows!

(**CHEETS** *franticly runs around.*)

CHEETS. The Queen! The Queen!

(He runs to **EMMA***.)*

Emma! The Queen cometh!

(**QUEEN CLEO** *and her* **HANDMAIDENS** *enter.* **CHEETS** *runs around doing cartwheels and somersaults, bumping into everyone.*)

The Queen! The Queen!

QUEEN CLEO. Cheets!

STARE. Who?

(**CHEETS** *ignores the Queen.*)

QUEEN CLEO. CHEETS!

> (**CHEETS** *is still running amok.* **CLEO** *snaps her fingers.*)

Cheets! Time OUT!

> (**CHEETS** *freezes in mid-run.*)

At last. Some peace and quiet. Donald, we are concerned about Emma. Is there any word?

> (**DONALD** *bows deeply.*)

DONALD. Good day, my Queen. No, we are still trying to find a way. May I present someone to you?

QUEEN CLEO. Yes, by all means.

STARE. Who?

DONALD. *(to* **STARE***)* The Queen has not met Emma's mother, Stare. Your Majesty, may I present Lady Rose.

QUEEN CLEO. Ah, at last. Emma's Mother. We have heard how beautiful you are, Lady Rose.

> (**ROSE** *curtsies deeply.*)

ROSE. Your Majesty! I too have heard about you. You are even more lovely than Emma described to me.

QUEEN CLEO. Emma spoke of us?

ROSE. Only in story form, your Grace. I had no idea all of this existed…*(laughing)* I only believed that my daughter had a wonderful imagination.

DONALD. My Queen, I was just telling Lady Rose the story of Hazard and Emma and Prince Rainier. Would you continue it?

ROSE. Yes, if it pleases your Majesty.

QUEEN CLEO. Very well. But, Lady Rose, this story cannot be told outside our forest. May we have your word?

ROSE. *(with a curtsey)* Of course, Your Majesty.

QUEEN CLEO. Very good. You see, Homer has been…

ROSE. Homer, your Majesty??

> (**CLEO** *laughs.*)

QUEEN CLEO. Yes, Lord Hazard. He hates it when we call him by his first name. Hazard and our court have coexisted for centuries and we bump along fairly well together. That is, until he gets out of hand like now. But, let us give you some history...

(Everyone loves a good story. They settle down to listen. **CHEETS** *struggles and tries to speak.* **CLEO** *crosses to him.)*

Ah, Cheets. Have you had a long enough time out to start behaving yourself?

(CHEETS *wiggles and tries to answer.)*

All right, you will sit quietly while we tell Lady Rose the story...

(CLEO *snaps her fingers.* **CHEETS** *starts running around.)*

CHEETS. Cheets is free! Free! Cheets loves a story.

QUEEN CLEO. Cheets!

(CHEETS *runs and sits down.)*

CHEETS. Cheets is a good elf.

(CLEO *crosses and sits. Her* **HANDMAIDENS** *gather around her.)*

QUEEN CLEO. Once upon a time, many centuries ago, there was a beloved King. He married Lady Roselyn **(ROSE** *reacts)* and they had a son, Prince Rainier. They ruled their people with kindness and generosity. One day Hazard saw Queen Roselyn and fell in love with her. He had to have her. But Roselyn wanted nothing to do with Hazard and sent him away. You see, she loved her husband-king and her son very much. Then one day the King fell ill and sadly, he died. Roselyn was deeply grieved but had her son to care for. After a time, Hazard came and tried to court the Queen. There were rumors that Hazard had something to do with the King's death. Roselyn sent him away a final time. Hazard was very angry.

(CHEETS *jumps up.)*

CHEETS. Cheets knows! Let me! Let me tell Lady Rose what happened next!

QUEEN CLEO. You have our permission, Cheets, but you must stay calm. No jumping around and running.

(**CHEETS** *'walks' around to everyone telling the story.*)

CHEETS. Hazard was so angry that he rained down spiders and frogs and bugs onto the earth. Volcanos erupted, seas boiled. He bewitched Prince Rainier and turned him into a Unicorn. Hazard banished him forever and ever...He could never go home again. He...

STARE. Who?

CHEETS. (*embroidering outrageously on the story*) Prince Rainier! He got scabs all over his body...his hair fell out... he got cavities in his teeth...his tail fell off...he got *bad breath*...

QUEEN CLEO. That's enough, Cheets. (*beat*) And the prince was banished to our forest in the form of Rainey, the Unicorn.

ROSE. What happened to the Queen...Roselyn?

QUEEN CLEO. She died of a broken heart.

ROSE. And the bewitched Prince? What happened to him?

QUEEN CLEO. But, my dear, don't you know? Emma saved him and broke Hazard's curse.

(*The* **QUEEN, ROSE, DONALD, CHEETS** *and all the others look at the web.*)

Scene Two

(AT RISE: **PATSY** *knits and munches.* **EMMA** *sits near the web wall.)*

PATSY. Won't be long now, little girl. As soon as Hazard conducts his 'business' you'll be free…maybe.

EMMA. Why are you so mean? I can't say that I particularly *like* spiders but I've never hurt one.

PATSY. It's all about supply and demand. As long has Lord Hazard has these delicious bugs for me *(giggles)* I have a strong web for him.

*(***MAX*** *bounds onto the stage. He runs straight to* **EMMA.***)*

EMMA. Max! How are you boy? I wish you could hear me.

MAX. Hi Emma. I can hear you. I can see you too…

EMMA. Oh, Max…

(She reaches through the webbing and hugs **MAX.***)*

How is this possible?

MAX. Don't know. Maybe it's because we're so loyal and loving…gives us special powers. What do you think?

EMMA. *(hugging* **MAX***)* Oh, I don't care! It's just so good to see you.

*(***MAX*** *pants, and grins and wiggles and wags with joy. He begins to chew at the web.)*

PATSY. Hey! You're not supposed to do that. I'm telling…

MAX. Oh be quiet, you…you…arachnid, you!

PATSY. Who are you calling an arachnid? No reason to use bad language! I'm a banana spider.

MAX. You big bug eater! Moth muncher!

EMMA. Max, hush now. Just ignore her. Patsy, I think you missed a stitch…

PATSY. I did? Oh, no! Look what you made me do you furry bag of bones!

STARE. Who?

EMMA. Tell me, Max, how is Mother doing? Is she okay?

MAX. Yes, she's happier knowing that while you are being held captive at least you have all these friends around you. But, she still cries at night when she thinks no one can hear her.

EMMA. Oh no.

MAX. It's all right…I climb up in her lap and give her doggy kisses.

EMMA. *(She hugs MAX.)* My favorite thing…doggy kisses.

(Suddenly clashes of thunder are heard and HAZARD arrives alone still dressed for his business meeting. MAX turns and growls. What few woodland creatures are seen fade back into the forest.)

HAZARD. Hello all! Patsy, is our little captive behaving herself?

STARE. Who?

HAZARD. Quiet, you bag of wet feathers!

STARE. WHO?

PATSY. Yes, Lord Hazard. *(beat)* Thank you for the new batch of lightning bugs. Delicious. That mangy fur trap there can see and talk to the girl.

HAZARD. Interesting. But the mutt can't talk to Lady Rose so we're good.

EMMA. Don't be too certain of that, Hazard.

(rubbing his hands together)

HAZARD. Well, now to business.

ROSE *(off)* Max. Here boy, come here, Max.

(ROSE enters.)

ROSE. Max! Here boy!

(Ignoring HAZARD, ROSE crosses to MAX and EMMA. She squats down by MAX.)

There you are, you bad boy. *(Beat. Looking inside the web.)* Do you think Emma is there, Max?

(MAX wags and squirms.)

HAZARD. Good day, my Lady.

(**ROSE** *rises and turns to* **HAZARD**. *She is cool.*)

ROSE. Lord Hazard.

(*Three* **MEN** *enter dressed as developers.*)

DEVELOPER #1. Mr. Hazard! Good to see you.

(*They all shake* **HAZARD**'*s hand.*)

HAZARD. Likewise. May I present a friend, Lady…er..I mean, Miss Rose.

ROSE. How do you do?

DEVELOPER #1. Pleasure, little lady.

ROSE. I must go. Please excuse me. Come, Max.

(**MAX** *stays by* **EMMA** *and whines.*)

Max, come!

(**MAX** *reluctantly crosses to* **ROSE**'*s side. They exit.*)

DEVELOPER #2. What a looker!

DEVELOPER #3. Yeah!

HAZARD. That's enough! What have you brought me?

(*The* **MEN** *open what appear to be land maps and architectural plans.*)

DEVELOPER #1. We've completed the plans. This first batch are the streets and infrastructure of the development. And these (*He opens another set.*) are the architectural drawings for 400 houses.

DEVELOPER #2. There will be green space but about eighty percent of this (*indicates the forest*) 'jungle' will be gone.

(*with pride as if destroying the forest completely and using the lumber was good management*)

DEVELOPER #3. We figure we can recycle about forty percent of the lumber. Cut our building costs.

(**EMMA** *is shaking the web and calling out silently.*)

HAZARD. Sounds good. When can you start?

DEVELOPER #3. As soon as you sign the contracts.

DEVELOPER #1. And we've saved the best for last. The name of the development!

STARE. Who?

DEVELOPER #2. You're gonna love it.

HAZARD. Just as long as it isn't something gooey like 'Whispering Plantations'.

DEVELOPER #1. We're calling it, HAZARD'S WOOD.

STARE. WHO??

(**EMMA** *continues to silently react.*)

HAZARD. 'Hazard's Wood'. hmm…yes…'Hazard's Wood'. I like it!

DEVELOPER #1. Thought you would. *(beat)* Now! I've written down the purchase price we are offering you, Mr. Hazard, on this piece of paper.

(*He hands a scrap of paper to* **HAZARD** *who reads it.* **HAZARD** *stands still and stares at the three* **DEVELOPERS** *until they start to squirm.*)

DEVELOPER #2. That's just the opening offer, you understand.

HAZARD. I would hope so. I'll let you know tomorrow. Same time, same place.

(*The* **DEVELOPERS** *exit.*)

(**HAZARD** *turns to* **EMMA.**)

Twenty million, brat. That's what *your* forest is worth. Whadda' think of that?

(*Laughing* **HAZARD** *starts to exit, he stuffs the scrap of paper into his suit pocket but misses and the paper falls to the forest floor.*)

'Hazard's Wood', yeah, I like it. Has a nice ring to it.

(*He exits.*)

Scene Three

(*AT RISE:* **EMMA** *sits behind the web. The forest is quiet with the exception of little faeries and creatures creeping about.*)

(**CHEETS** *runs in, shouting. He is waving a large beautiful carrot, his favorite.*)

CHEETS. The carrots are ready! The carrots are delicious! Cheets loves his carrots.

(*He stops in front of* **EMMA.**)

Look, Emma! Isn't it beautiful? (*takes a bite*) And so good! Yum!

(**EMMA** *tries to get* **CHEETS**' *attention.*)

What!?

STARE. Who?

CHEETS. What, Emma?

(**EMMA** *begins to pantomime the scrap of paper that still lies on the ground unnoticed.*)

Okay, I can finish my carrot later. Two words. First word. Three syllables?

(**EMMA** *acts out the word 'important'.*)

Significant.

(**EMMA** *shakes her head.*)

No, too many syllables. Crucial. Vital. No? Too few. Essential? Critical?

(**CHEETS** *is jumping up and down in frustration.*)

This is a very difficult one, Emma.

(**EMMA** *pantomimes first syllable. Herself as in 'I'.*)

Okay. First syllable. You. No? I?

(**EMMA** *tries to stretch it out.*)

I? I'd? I've? NO? What is it?

(**CHEETS** *paces up and down, muttering. He whirls back to* **EMMA.**)

CHEETS. *(cont.)* *I'M* ! It's I'm, isn't it?

> *(He does a victory dance.* **EMMA** *waves her hands to get* **CHEETS**' *attention again.)*

Second syllable.

> *(***EMMA** *pantomimes a boat docking in a 'port'. She is unsuccessful.* **THOMAS** *enters and crosses to* **CHEETS**.*)*

Car? Bicycle? No...

> *(***THOMAS** *doesn't know what* **CHEETS** *is doing and is randomly trying to help.)*

THOMAS. Ship?

> *(***EMMA** *motions that* **THOMAS** *almost has it right. She indicates something smaller than a ship.)*

What are we doing, Cheets?

CHEETS. Emma is trying to tell me something and it's very hard. She seems to be driving something. It's the second syllable. The second syllable is close to a...what you said, Thomas, 'a ship'.

THOMAS. Stow the gear! Clear the decks! she must mean a 'boat'.

> *(Finger to nose,* **EMMA** *gestures jumping out of the boat and tying up at the dock.)*

CHEETS. Now she's jumped out of the boat and is doing something...

THOMAS. Make fast. Tie 'er down! There's a storm a'brewin'!

CHEETS. Yes! Yes! she just tied the boat up. But, where?

THOMAS. The dock?

> *(***EMMA** *indicates not just a dock but the whole port.)*

CHEETS. No, something more, something bigger.

THOMAS. Safe harbor! What every sailor needs.

> *(***EMMA** *shakes her head 'no' but that* **THOMAS** *is close.)*

CHEETS. No, not 'harbor'...give me something else, Thomas. Hurry!

THOMAS. Shiver me timbers! Hmm...not 'harbor'... Anchorage? Wharf? Marina?...Quay.

(**EMMA** *shakes her head.* **THOMAS** *begins his plodding pace across the stage towards the scrap of paper. He spots the paper and heads straight for it, muttering seafaring utterances.*)

THOMAS. *(cont.)* It brings to mind a safe harbor off of Africa. A lovely little port.

(**EMMA** *jumps up and down and points at* **THOMAS.**)

CHEETS. Thomas! What did you just say?

(**THOMAS** *stops and turns back.*)

THOMAS. Hmm? You mean just now. I was remembering Africa. A harbor there, snug it was.

(**CHEETS** *looks at* **EMMA**; *she shakes her head and motions for more.*)

CHEETS. No, that's not it, Thomas. Emma says you said something else.

THOMAS. No, no. I was just remembering what a lovely little port it was.

(**EMMA** *jumps up and down, excited and putting her finger on her nose.*)

CHEETS. That's it, Thomas! 'Port'. The second syllable is 'port. Now, let's put it together…'I'm' 'port' ?? *(beat)* Emma, that makes no sense.

(**EMMA** *motions to string it out.*)

I'm port….Import…yes?

(**EMMA** *places her finger on her nose several times. She gestures a tent shape with her hands.* **THOMAS** *continues his cross towards the paper.*)

Church steeple? No?…House?…Roof? …TENT!! Is it a tent? Yes? Im…port…tent.
IMPORTANT!!! Is that the first word?

(**EMMA** *nods and touches her finger to her nose once again. She pantomimes second word, two syllables, reading, writing, and paper.*)

CHEETS. *(cont.)* Second word, two syllables? Reading? No. WRITING! Yes! No?

(**EMMA** *slaps the invisible paper she has written on.*)

Oh! Paper?

(*Meanwhile,* **THOMAS** *has discovered the paper and decides it is something to eat. He begins to slowly munch away on it.* **EMMA** *makes frantic motions to* **CHEETS** *to look at* **THOMAS** *and the paper he is eating.*)

Ah! Important paper! That's it, isn't it? Cheets is so smart! Cheets is a good elf. Cheets has a bigger brain… What, Emma? Throw the paper away…

(**CHEETS** *finally looks around and sees* **THOMAS** *calmly eating a paper.* **CHEETS** *runs over to* **THOMAS** *and makes a "first base slide" at* **THOMAS**'s *head and the paper.*)

THOMAS!

STARE. Who?

THOMAS. What!?

CHEETS. Don't eat that! Give it here!

(**THOMAS** *spits it out.* **CHEETS** *smooths out the paper and wipes it off.*)

Eeeww…turtle spit!

THOMAS. Stow your portion! Steady as she goes, mate. There's more chow in the galley.

CHEETS. I'm sorry, Thomas, but this isn't food. It's the 'important paper' that Emma was trying to tell us about.

THOMAS. Well, shred my sails and call me a stink pot. What do you make of that?

CHEETS. Now, let's see what this is…

(**CHEETS** *looks at* **EMMA**.)

Twenty. Oh my, look at all these zeros…too many for Cheets. Emma, do you know what all these 'zeros' mean?

(**CHEETS** *shows her the paper.* **EMMA** *repeats her pantomime of* **HAZARD**, *and hammering wood and cutting.*)

CHEETS. *(cont.)* Hazard is connected to this paper, Emma? The forest, cutting, oh dear, oh dear…

THOMAS. We're in for a bad blow…Reef the sails.

(**EMMA** *gestures that* **CHEETS** *should get her mother.*)

CHEETS. Lady Rose. Yes, Emma, that's who we should show this to. Let Cheets think…Thomas! Sound the alarm, gather everyone here in two…*(considers how slow* **THOMAS** *is)* …No, make that three hours. Cheets will tell Donald to bring Lady Rose here.

(**THOMAS** *begins to exit.*)

THOMAS. Aye, aye, Matey. Sound the alarm, fire below decks. Man the buckets, make that gear secure…don't be bamboozled by 'em…

(*He exits.*)

Scene Four

(*AT RISE: Everyone has gathered near* **PATSY**'s *web for a meeting.*)

(**CHEETS** *is centerstage.* **EMMA** *is near the web wall.* **THOMAS** *is upstage near* **PATSY**. *All the woodland creatures and faeries are in attendance.* **PATSY** *is frantically knitting.*)

PATSY. I'm telling! You can't have this meeting without Lord Hazard.

CHEETS. Pipe down, Bananas! Mind your own beeswax!

THOMAS. Blustery wind bag! Don't allow 'em on my ship!

STARE. Who?

THOMAS. Patsy!

CHEETS. Bananas!

PATSY. Stop calling me that! My name is Patsy.

(*No one pays* **PATSY** *any attention.* **DONALD** *enters escorting* **ROSE**. **MAX** *is at her side and runs ahead to sit by* **EMMA**. **CHEETS** *rushes over to* **ROSE**.)

CHEETS. Lady Rose, hurry, I have terrible news. Terrible!!

DONALD. Cheets! Calm down and tell us why you have called us all here.

ROSE. Is it about Emma, darling Cheets? Is she safe? Is she still there? (*indicating the web*)

PATSY. Of course, she's still there. No one, but *no one* escapes my web.

CHEETS. Yes, she's there, Lady. But Emma has some terrible news and I have the proof.

(**CHEETS** *walks around, all puffed up.*)

DONALD. Enough with the mystery, Cheets! Tell us.

CHEETS. Well! Emma heard Hazard making a deal to destroy our beautiful forest. He is selling it to what the earthlings call, 'developers'. Very bad men! Very bad!

ROSE. He can't *do* that. The forest belongs to my family. It's part of our farm.

DONALD. Cheets. How do you know this?

CHEETS. She told me with sign language…Cheets is very smart…Cheets learned Emma's language *(He snaps his fingers.)* in no time.

DONALD. You say you have proof of this?

CHEETS. Thomas almost ate my proof.

ROSE. I'm certain Thomas didn't mean to, did you Thomas?

THOMAS. It looked like seaweed off the coast of Japan…

CHEETS. Cheets has the proof right here. *(waving the scrap of paper in the air)* Cheets can't understand all these zeros…Cheets is very smart, big brain…

DONALD. Never mind that now, Cheets. Let me see.

*(**DONALD**, **CHEETS**, and **ROSE** all gather around to look. **DONALD** reads aloud.)*

C.R.O.O.K.S. *(spelling it out)* Crooks Construction? Offering to buy the land to build four hundred houses. Twenty thousand?

*(Slowly **ROSE** takes the paper from **DONALD**'s hand. She looks at everyone.)*

ROSE. No, Donald. This number is twenty million. Crooks Construction is offering Hazard twenty million for our forest.

THOMAS. Shiver me timbers!

PATSY. That buys a lotta' bugs.

*(Everyone speaks at once. All the faeries and woodland creatures run around, crying and holding each other. **ROSE** sits near **EMMA**. **CHEETS** and **DONALD** sit on toad stools. Suddenly bells and horns announce the arrival of **QUEEN CLEO** and her entourage.)*

QUEEN CLEO. Silence! Whatever is the matter? We demand silence!

STARE. Who?

*(**DONALD** rises and crosses to **CLEO**.)*

DONALD. The most terrible news, my Queen. Hazard is selling our forest to…developers. *(He says 'developers' like it's a bad word.)*

*(**CHEETS** jumps up and runs to the **QUEEN**. He veers off and runs around the stage.)*

CHEETS. Four hundred houses! Roads! Those awful stinky machines! MY CARROT PATCH WILL BE RUINED!

(**CHEETS** *realizing his carrots are at risk and he runs off.*)

MY CARROTS!!

QUEEN CLEO. How do you know this? Hazard cannot do that!

DONALD. Emma told Cheets she overheard the plans. And then Cheets and Thomas found this…

(**DONALD** *hands her the scrap of paper.*)

QUEEN CLEO. Hazard goes too far this time! We will not tolerate his insolence!

(**CHEETS** *runs back on.*)

CHEETS. Hazard is coming. Watch out! It's Hazard! Wait until Cheets gives him what for…Cheets is very brave…

QUEEN CLEO. Cheets, do we need a time out?

CHEETS. No, my Queen. Cheets will behave. Cheets is a good elf.

(**HAZARD** *arrives amongst thunder and lightning and his* **HENCHMEN**.)

HAZARD. Queeny, how goes you?

QUEEN CLEO. Homer! What is this story we have been told?

(**HAZARD** *winces at the use of his first name.*)

HAZARD. Cleo! I have told you not to call me that. I am the GREAT HAZARD, Lord of the Underworld.

QUEEN CLEO. Very well, Hazard. We want to know what you are up to.

HAZARD. Whatever do you mean, Cleo?

THOMAS. I don't like the cut of his jib.

STARE. Who?

DONALD. Not now, Stare.

QUEEN CLEO. We have heard of a sale you are negotiating with Crooks? Construction?

(**CLEO** *jabs the air with the piece of paper.*)

HAZARD. I'm sure I don't know what you're talking about… who is Crooks Construction?

(**CLEO** *gives the paper to* **HAZARD**.)

Oh, this? Just exploring my options, my dear Queen. Nothing to worry about.

QUEEN CLEO. *(sputtering)* NOTHING. TO. WORRY. ABOUT. How dare you…

(**ROSE** *rises and crosses to* **CLEO** *and* **HAZARD**.)

ROSE. Queen Cleo, if I may…I would ask that I be allowed to discuss this with Lord Hazard.

QUEEN CLEO. We grant you our permission.

(**CLEO** *sits in her chair, surrounded by her* **HANDMAID-ENS**. *The faeries and woodland creatures all creep out to watch and listen.*)

ROSE. Lord Hazard, a word if you will.

HAZARD. Anything for you, my love. How may I be of service, Lady Roselyn?

ROSE. I am *not* your Lady Roselyn. And, I am certainly not your 'love'. I am simply Rose.

HAZARD. Ah, Queen of my heart. I beg to differ.

(**ROSE** *sighs and realizes that she is not going to win.*)

ROSE. Fine! If you want to think of me as Roselyn, what's in a name? I have a counter offer to present to you.

(All gasp.)

HAZARD. Ah…this could be interesting. Please, my Lady, have a seat and we will talk.

(**HAZARD** *leads* **ROSE**, *by the hand, to a toad stool and sits at her feet.*)

Now, my love, what did you have in mind?

ROSE. As you might remember, my Lord, Queen Cleo bestowed the forest upon Emma and I to show her appreciation for Emma's success on her quest.

(**HAZARD** *speaks sharply, irritated to be reminded of his past failures.*)

HAZARD. Yes, yes!! Get on with it.

ROSE. Did you know that my farm is a larger parcel of land than that of the forest?

HAZARD. No, I did not know that. That's very interesting. What are you saying, my Roselyn?

ROSE. What if I trade you our farm for the forest? It has much better views, already has been cleared, has utilities. It would save you money.

(*Everyone reacts.* **EMMA** *is frantic.*)

QUEEN CLEO. Lady Rose, you cannot give up your home…

STARE. Who?

THOMAS. Swing the lead. We're in the shallows.

DONALD. Oh, my Lady, don't. The farm means everything to you and Emma.

(**CHEETS** *crosses to* **EMMA.**)

CHEETS. Emma! Did you hear? Your mother is going to sell the farm to Hazard. Oh dear! The garden!

(*as he exits*)

THE CARROTS!! THE CARROTS!!

(**ROSE** *holds up her hands for quiet.*)

ROSE. Well, my Lord, what say you?

HAZARD. What do you want in return, my Lady?

ROSE. You set my daughter free. You promise to never touch the forest again. In return you can have the farm and all the lands that are mine.

HAZARD. An interesting offer to be sure, my love. But, not good enough.

(*All react with groans, sighs.*)

ROSE. Very well. What else do you want?

HAZARD. For you, my Lady, my Queen, to at least consider my suit. Let me court you…

ROSE. Never!

HAZARD. Pray, let me finish, Lady. If after three earth months, you do not love me, I will leave forever.

(*Beat.* **ROSE** *considers.*)

ROSE. Very well, Lord Hazard. I think I can tolerate you for three months. Now, set my daughter free at once!

HAZARD. My love, you have had the power to set her free all this time…

ROSE. Me? What? How?

STARE. Who?

DONALD. What are you talking about, Hazard?

PATSY. Wait! What about my bugs??

(**CHEETS** *runs back on.*)

CHEETS. Emma is to be freed! Hoorah for Emma! Freedom for Emma!

STARE. Who?

HAZARD. The golden scissors, there in your pocket…

(**ROSE** *reaches into her pocket slowly and draws out a pair of golden scissors.*)

ROSE. These were not here before.

HAZARD. Perhaps. *(beat)* But they will cut the web and set your daughter free.

PATSY. No! No cutting! Not my beautiful web. You can't. She's mine.

ROSE. Cheets, I think you should have the honor of setting Emma free.

(*She holds out scissors to* **CHEETS**. *He takes them and dashes about the stage with them.*)

CHEETS. Cheets gets the honor! Cheets is such a brave, good elf…

STARE. Who?

QUEEN CLEO. Cheets, don't run with scissors in your hand. You'll get hurt!

(**CHEETS** *stalks over to the web as if he is a great hunter.*)

PATSY. Ha! I can weave and repair my web faster than you can cut.

(**PATSY** *knits furiously.* **CHEETS** *begins to cut the web. He does not succeed at first as* **PATSY** *is knitting faster than he can cut.* **EMMA** *waits impatiently on the other side, watching* **PATSY** *and then* **CHEETS**.)

CHEETS. Lady Rose, I cannot cut it fast enough! What shall I do?

(**QUEEN CLEO** *snaps her fingers and one of her* **HAND-MAIDENS** *begins a slow dance crossing the stage. She holds a long pole from which flies, at the end of a ribbon,a beautiful butterfly. The* **HANDMAIDEN** *positions the flight of the butterfly over* **PATSY.** *She is immediately distracted from her knitting by the thoughts of this delicacy.*)

PATSY. Yum! Look at that! Come here my little pretty.

(**PATSY** *stops knitting to focus on the bug.* **CHEETS** *is now making progress cutting the web.* **EMMA** *is freed and runs to her mother.* **ROSE** *embraces her. Just as* **PATSY** *thinks she will have the butterfly, it flies off as the* **HAND-MAIDEN** *exits with the pole.*)

Wait! Come back here! *(to everyone)* You tricked me!

ROSE. My darling girl. At last you are safe.

(**DONALD** *and* **CHEETS** *cross to* **EMMA.** *She hugs them both.* **MAX** *is jumping around* **EMMA.**)

CHEETS. Cheets is brave, Emma. Cheets set you free. Cheets is such a good elf.

EMMA. Yes, Cheets. Thank you very much for helping me. You saved the forest, Cheets. *(Beat. Turns to* **DONALD.**) Oh, Donald, I've missed you…*(shy)* I mean, I've missed *everyone* so much. Thank you all for believing in me even though you couldn't see me.

(*Everyone shouts a 'hoorah' and dances around.*)

ROSE. Lord Hazard, you have kept your word.

(**HAZARD** *kneels before* **ROSE.**)

HAZARD. My love, my Roselyn. You have my word and my undying love. I would give you anything that you ask of me.

ROSE. You have given me my daughter, my Lord, that is enough.

(Everyone cheers. **CHEETS** *runs around doing cartwheels, somersaults.* **HAZARD** *rises and begins to cross the stage to exit.* **ROSE** *and* **EMMA** *embrace once again. As* **HAZARD** *exits, he stops and turns back to* **ROSE.***)*

HAZARD. Lady Roselyn.

ROSE. Yes, my Lord?

HAZARD. Just as I did not kill your husband-king those many centuries ago, I did not know that Emma was your daughter. I would never harm your child.

*(***HAZARD*** and* **ROSE** *look at each other. Everyone witnesses this moment in eternity. Several beats.)*

ROSE. I think I believe you, my Lord.

*(***HAZARD*** turns again as if to exit. He turns back.)*

HAZARD. One more thing, my love.

ROSE. Yes?

HAZARD. *(He smiles.)* The deal is off.

ROSE. What?!

DONALD. You can't do that, Hazard.

(running around in circles)

CHEETS. Pants on fire! Fibber! Hazard is a bad, bad man!

QUEEN CLEO. Hazard, what are you up to now?

STARE. Who?

THOMAS. It's an ill wind that blows. Still waters run deep! The ship's breaching!

*(***PATSY*** knits furiously.)*

PATSY. Where's that lovely bug gone to? Oh dear, look at my web.

HAZARD. QUIET!!
My lady, the deal is off in as much as your farm is concerned. If a man truly loves a woman, he does not take. He gives. The farm is yours, and of course, Emma's. This forest will be protected for all time. *(beat)*
Until we next meet, my love, Queen of my Heart.

*(He exits. The faeries and woodland creatures dance about. **EMMA** and **DONALD** and **CHEETS** dance with each other. **CLEO** sits smiling. **ROSE** stands, quietly, stunned.)*

(CURTAIN)

PRODUCTION NOTES

1. If possible, Thomas should wear a shell that Cheets can sit on and ride at their entrance. He should wear a white sailor's hat and a blue and white neck kerchief. "Foresail" is pronounced: 'fore sull.'

2. Patsy, the spider, should be able to knit or crochet shiny gossamer yarn the entire time. At the bottom of the piece she is knitting a long single strand should run to the web. Dark chocolate covered raisins and red M&M's work best for the 'bugs' she is eating.

3. The pantomime/charade is created when Cheets finds that he cannot hear Emma. No one can see or hear Emma except for Cheets, and later, Max. The author has included some simple 'charade' blocking. This would be a great opportunity for the theatre company to hold pantomime classes. Audience participation could be encouraged during the charades.

4. Queen Cleo speaks in the royal 'we.' The handmaidens of the Queen are dressed entirely in their 'color,' including their hands, feet, faces and hair.

5. The set and costume designs should take up most of the budget. The forest needs to be deep and mysterious and lush. The entire theatre can be part of the set; stage, aisles, and lobby. In that case, important entrances [with particular thought to the Queen and her entourage, Hazard, and his henchmen] could be made from the lobby and up/down the aisles, onto the stage.

6. Cheets should never be still except when the Queen, losing all patience, temporarily freezes him; giving him a 'time out.'

7. Max, the family dog should be portrayed much like the dog in the play *Sylvia*. Max can be erect, or down on all fours creating a dog with body movements. A caricature of a dog should be avoided. Max and Emma can see and talk with each other.

8. Rose and Hazard should be, if possible, cast by young adults so that the century long love story is believable.

9. Queen Cleo's chair should be a huge flower or something equally grand.

10. The discussion about 'who' and 'whom' and the grammatically correct application should be delivered with complete sincerity.

11. The scrap of paper with the purchase price on it should be large enough that Thomas can start to eat it and it still be legible.

12. When Cheets and Emma 'talk' the actors should only watch Cheets, never Emma.

If there are additional questions relating to the script, please contact the playwright at: www.writeratplay.com

NAUTICAL TERMS AND DEFINITIONS

Bad blow: A big storm.
Bamboozle: From the 17th century, it describes the Spanish custom of hoisting false flags to deceive [bamboozle] enemies at sea.
Breaching: When a ship is in danger of sinking.
Brig: Jail.
Chow: Food.
Crow's Nest: Is at the top of the mast and used for a look out.
Cut of his jib: A jib sail is triangular in shape.
Dance the hempen jig: To hang someone.
Freebooters: Pirates.
Galley: The kitchen on a boat.
Leeward: The side the wind blows less or not at all.
Poop deck: The roof of a cabin and is found aft [the rear] on a ship.
Port side: The left side.
Prepare to be boarded: A forceful coming aboard another ship.
Reef the sails: Reducing the amount of sail that is used.
Shiver me timbers: In a storm the timbers holding the ship together would 'shiver' and shake.
Steady as she blows: refers to it requiring more than one sailor to hold the wheel and keep the ship steady on course in a heavy wind.
Stink pot: a power boat.
Stow your portion: Saving your meal (dinner).
Swing the lead: lead weight swung from a line into the water to measure the depth.
Windward: The side the wind blows hardest.

Also by
Trisha Sugarek...

Emma and the Lost Unicorn

The Guyer Girls

Please visit our website **bakersplays.com** for complete
descriptions and licensing information

OTHER TITLES AVAILABLE FROM BAKER'S PLAYS

THE ELVES AND THE SHOEMAKER

Kristin Walter

Comedy / 3f, 2m / multiple settings

Unfortunately, Eric, the lone shoemaker of Grimmsville, makes shoes that are miserably uncomfortable and impossible to walk in...leaving a lot of barefoot villagers and Eric without a means to provide for his family. While his wife tries to be supportive, his daughter Shannon just can't take it anymore! Sitting alone in the woods pondering her family's fate, Shannon is confronted by a stranger who offers her the deal of a lifetime... in exchange for her torturous pair of shoes, she is given a magical medallion that holds "the charm of the elves." Wanting to help her family, Shannon tries the chant. Her words beckon a pair of elves that show up night after night at the shoemaker's home creating the most fabulous shoes EVER! With his shoes now wanted throughout the land, Eric and his family have more gold than they can count. But they quickly begin to realize that all the money in the world doesn't necessarily buy happiness.

"...the script by Kristin Walter is a joy - true to the original story, but with enough clever asides to keep the parents in the audience laughing along with the kids."
- *nytheatre.com*

"Walter is a clever playwright. She masterfully writes one line for the children to enjoy and follows it up with a quick-witted one that seems to nudge the parent in the rib."
- *Off-Off Broadway Review*